Winnie-the-Pooh's
Teatime Cookbook

INSPIRED BY
A. A. MILNE

Winnie-the-Pooh's Teatime Cookbook

WITH DECORATIONS BY
ERNEST H. SHEPARD

Dutton Children's Books
NEW YORK

Library of Congress Cataloging-in-Publication Data
Winnie-the-Pooh's teatime cookbook / inspired by A. A. Milne; with decorations by Ernest H. Shepard.
p. cm.
Includes excerpts from stories by A. A. Milne. Includes index.
Summary: Discusses the phenomenon of afternoon tea and provides recipes for muffins, pastries, and
other appropriate fare, punctuated by quotations from the works of A. A. Milne.
ISBN 0-525-45135-8
1. Afternoon teas—Juvenile literature. [1. Afternoon teas. 2. Cookery. 3. Literary cookbooks.] I. Milne,
A. A. (Alan Alexander), 1882–1956. II. Shepard, Ernest H. (Ernest Howard), 1879–1976, ill.
TX736.W56 1993
641.5'3—dc20 92-35650 CIP AC

Published in the United States 1993 by Dutton Children's Books, a division of Penguin Books USA Inc.
375 Hudson Street, New York, New York 10014

Printed in Hong Kong
Designed by Joseph Rutt
Additional illustrations by E. Kwei
5 6 7 8 9 10

Contents

≈ ≈

A Word about Tea

By-and-by Pooh and Piglet went on again.
Christopher Robin was at home by this time, because it was
the afternoon, and he was so glad to see them that they stayed there until
very nearly tea-time, and then they had a Very Nearly tea, which is one you
forget about afterwards, and hurried on to Pooh Corner, so as to see Eeyore
before it was too late to have a Proper Tea with Owl.

The House At Pooh Corner

6

There is a certain time of day when lunch is a distant memory and dinner seems very far off indeed. For a bear like Pooh who enjoys a little smackerel of something, teatime is the perfect invention. All activities stop, and the table is laden with delicious things to eat. Pooh's honey can be accompanied by sandwiches, scones, cookies, cakes, and a nice pot of tea.

The idea of appeasing late-afternoon hunger in this delightful way is credited to Anna, seventh duchess of Bedford. This nineteenth-century English lady grew impatient waiting for the dinner hour and asked servants to bring tea and refreshments to her room each day at four o'clock. She invited friends to join her in this small feast. As word of her activities spread, afternoon tea became the fashion and a lasting tradition.

Amid the inviting array of sweets and savories is the essential ingredient in this late-afternoon meal — the proper pot of tea. It should be prepared as follows:

Fill a kettle with cold water and bring it to a boil. Meanwhile, add a little hot water to a clean teapot to warm it. Swirl the water around the pot, then pour it out. Now add the tea to the pot, 1 teaspoon for each cup to be served and 1 for the pot. When the water in the kettle has reached a galloping boil, pour it into the teapot. Stir the mixture once, cover, and let the tea steep for 5 minutes.

To serve, pour a little milk into each cup, if desired. Then pour the tea through a strainer. Sugar or honey can then be added.

Young tea drinkers may prefer tea weakened with extra milk, or decaffeinated tea can be offered. Cocoa, hot cider, and warm milk with honey and vanilla are good alternative teatime beverages.

If a cooler drink is called for, try banana malts or orange milk mix.

A Word to Young Cooks

Some of the recipes in this book require the use of knives and other sharp utensils and appliances, as well as the stove and oven. Ask for adult supervision when these items are needed, and follow a few safety guidelines: Use pot holders when handling anything hot; always turn pan or skillet handles toward the back of the stove; cut away from yourself when using a vegetable peeler.

Be sure to read each recipe carefully before beginning, and take each step slowly. This will help prevent accidents and make your time in the kitchen more enjoyable.

8

☙ WARM MILK WITH HONEY AND VANILLA ❧

4 cups milk (whole or low fat)
3 tablespoons honey
½ teaspoon vanilla extract

Combine milk, honey, and vanilla in a saucepan and heat over medium flame until milk is warmed through. Do not boil. *Makes 4 one-cup servings.*

☙ BANANA MALT ❧

4 cups milk (whole or low fat)
6 tablespoons malt
1 ripe banana, peeled

Place milk, malt, and banana in blender and whip until light and frothy. *Makes 4 one-cup servings.*

☙ ORANGE MILK ❧

2 cups milk (whole or low fat)
2 cups orange juice

Place milk and juice in blender and whip until smooth and frothy. *Makes 4 one-cup servings.*

9

❧ Breads and Toasts ❧

Pooh always liked a little something at
eleven o'clock in the morning, and he was very glad to
see Rabbit getting out the plates and mugs; and when Rabbit said,
"Honey or condensed milk with your bread?"
he was so excited that he said, "Both," and then,
so as not to seem greedy, he added,
"but don't bother about the bread, please."
Winnie-the-Pooh

⌢ SANDWICH BREAD ⌢

1 package active dry yeast
2 cups warm water
3 teaspoons sugar
4 cups all-purpose flour
1½ tablespoons salt
butter, for buttering bowl

Pour yeast into ½ cup of the warm water, add sugar, stir, and set aside for 5 minutes. Put flour in a bowl, add salt, and blend. Add yeast mixture and water and mix with your hands until dough forms a ball. Add more flour or water as necessary. Move dough to a floured surface and knead at least 5 minutes. Butter a clean bowl, roll dough in buttered bowl to coat thoroughly, cover bowl with plastic wrap, and leave dough to rise in a warm, draft-free place for 1 to 1½ hours. After dough has risen, punch it down, knead again for about 3 minutes, and place in a greased 9 × 5 × 3-inch loaf pan. Let rise again for about 1 hour. Bake in preheated 400°F oven for 35 to 40 minutes. Bread is

12

done when it sounds hollow when tapped. Allow to cool in pan under a towel.

For whole-wheat bread, substitute 2 cups of whole-wheat flour for 2 cups of the all-purpose flour.

⌒ SODA BREAD ⌒

4 cups all-purpose flour, sifted
1 teaspoon salt
¼ cup sugar
1½ teaspoons baking powder
¼ cup butter (½ stick)
2 cups raisins
1⅓ cups buttermilk
1 egg
1 teaspoon baking soda
2 tablespoons honey
sugar, for decoration

Preheat oven to 425°F. Sift together flour, salt, sugar, and baking powder. Rub in butter until coarse mixture forms. Add raisins. In a small bowl, blend buttermilk, egg, baking soda, and honey. Add gradually to flour mixture, stirring until a dough forms. Turn dough out on a floured board and knead gently several times. Shape into a ball. Place on an ungreased cookie sheet. Sprinkle lightly with sugar and cut a deep cross into the top, about halfway through dough ball. Bake for 45 minutes. Cool on a wire rack under a towel.

14

⌇ Oatmeal Honey Bread ⌇

2 yeast cakes
1 cup lukewarm water
2 cups boiling water
1 cup oatmeal
1 cup butter (2 sticks)
½ cup honey
1 tablespoon cinnamon
1 tablespoon salt
2 eggs
6½ cups all-purpose flour

Add yeast to lukewarm water and stir until dissolved. Mix together boiling water, oatmeal, butter, honey, cinnamon, and salt in a large bowl and let cool. Mix in yeast and eggs. Sift in the flour one cup at a time and beat well. With floured hands, knead the mixture in bowl into a soft dough. Cover bowl with a clean dish towel and let dough rise in warm place until doubled in bulk (1 hour). Place on a floured board. Knead several times. Divide in half and place in 2 greased 9 × 5 × 3-inch loaf pans. Let rise in warm place until dough reaches the tops of the loaf pans (½ hour). Bake in preheated 375°F oven for 45 minutes. Allow to cool in pans under a towel.

15

⌐ BANANA BREAD ⌐

2 cups all-purpose flour
1 teaspoon baking soda
½ teaspoon salt
½ cup butter (1 stick)
1 cup sugar
2 eggs
2 ripe bananas, mashed
2 teaspoons lemon juice
½ cup milk

Preheat oven to 350°F. Sift together flour, baking soda, and salt. In another bowl, cream butter and sugar, then add eggs and bananas. Add lemon juice to milk. Add flour mixture and milk mixture to banana mixture alternately, ending with flour mixture. Pour into a buttered 9 × 5 × 3-inch loaf pan and bake for 50 minutes to 1 hour. Allow to cool in pan under a towel.

⌒ CHOCOLATE TEA BREAD ⌒

1 cup butter (2 sticks)
1¼ cups sugar
1 teaspoon vanilla extract
2 eggs
1 cup unsweetened cocoa
   powder
1 cup plain yogurt
1 teaspoon baking powder
½ teaspoon baking soda
¼ teaspoon salt
1¾ cups all-purpose flour
4 ounces semisweet chocolate
   chips

Preheat oven to 350°F. Mix together butter, sugar, and vanilla until light and fluffy. Add eggs one at a time, mixing rapidly. Gently mix in cocoa, yogurt, baking powder, baking soda, and salt. Then mix in flour until smooth. Add chocolate chips. Fold into a greased 9 × 5 × 3-inch loaf pan. Bake for 1 hour, or until toothpick inserted in top comes out clean. Allow to cool in pan under a towel.

☞ CHEESE AND APPLE TOASTS ☜

1 fresh tart apple
3 slices sandwich bread
1 cup grated cheddar cheese

Peel and core the apple and cut into ¼-inch-thick slices. Arrange apple slices on bread, cover with grated cheese, and toast in broiler or toaster oven until cheese melts. Cut into triangles and serve. *Makes 12 small toasts.*

☞ WELSH RABBIT ☜

2 tablespoons butter
½ cup cream
1 tablespoon prepared mustard
1 tablespoon prepared
  horseradish
1 teaspoon ground black pepper
1 cup grated cheddar cheese
8 slices sandwich bread

Mix together butter, cream, mustard, horse-radish, black pepper, and cheese in a saucepan. Place over low heat, stirring constantly until cheese has melted. Take pan off heat. Toast the bread. Pour cheese mixture over toast. Place under grill or broiler until skin forms. *Serves 4.*

⌒ SESAME TOASTS ⌒

2 *tablespoons butter, at room*
   temperature
4 *slices sandwich bread*
4 *tablespoons sesame seeds*

Spread butter on bread, sprinkle with sesame seeds, and broil or toast until lightly browned. Cut into quarters and serve warm. *Makes 16 small toasts.*

⌒ CINNAMON TOASTS ⌒

6 *teaspoons sugar*
¼ *teaspoon cinnamon*
4 *slices sandwich bread*
butter, for buttering toast

Mix sugar and cinnamon in a small bowl and set aside. Lightly toast the bread under the broiler. When golden, remove and butter. Spread the cinnamon-sugar mixture over buttered toast, return to the broiler, and broil *very* briefly, just until sugar is melted. Cut each piece of toast in half and serve. *Makes 8 toasts.*

Scones, Muffins, and Crumpets

I think I am a Muffin Man. I haven't got a
   bell,
I haven't got the muffin things that muffin people
   sell.

Now We Are Six

⌒ PLAIN SCONES ⌒

2 cups all-purpose flour
1 tablespoon baking powder
½ teaspoon salt
½ cup butter (1 stick)
2 tablespoons sugar
1 egg
⅓ cup buttermilk

Preheat oven to 450°F. Sift together flour, baking powder, and salt. Rub or cut in the butter as lightly as possible until the mixture resembles bread crumbs. Stir in sugar. Add the egg and bind mixture together with a fork. Gradually add the buttermilk to form a stiff dough.

Place dough on a floured board. Roll out to thickness of ¾ inch. Cut out circles using a 2½-inch cutter or cut into long triangles with a knife. Place scones 1 inch apart on greased cookie sheets. Bake for 10 to 12 minutes. Remove from oven and place on a wire rack. Cover with a cloth to keep the steam in. *Makes 12 scones.*

22

⌒ CHEESE SCONES ⌒

1 1/2 cups all-purpose flour
2 teaspoons baking powder
1 teaspoon dry mustard
1/2 teaspoon salt
1/4 cup butter (1/2 stick)
1 cup grated cheddar cheese
2 tablespoons grated Parmesan
  cheese
1 egg
1/2 cup buttermilk

Preheat oven to 400°F. Sift together flour, baking powder, dry mustard, and salt. Rub in butter with your fingers until mixture forms soft granules. Add cheeses and mix together. Break egg into buttermilk and beat with a fork to blend. Add this to flour mixture and stir until a dough forms. Knead dough several times on a floured board. Roll out to thickness of 1/2 inch. Cut into triangles or 3-inch circles. Place on an ungreased cookie sheet. Bake for 12 to 15 minutes. *Makes 12 scones.*

23

≈ OATMEAL RAISIN SCONES ≈

1 cup all-purpose flour
1 cup whole-wheat flour
1 teaspoon baking soda
½ teaspoon nutmeg
½ teaspoon cinnamon
3 tablespoons sugar
½ teaspoon salt
1 cup oatmeal
¾ cup butter (1½ sticks)
1 cup raisins
1 egg, separated
1 cup yogurt
sugar, for decoration

Preheat oven to 375°F. Sift together flours, baking soda, nutmeg, cinnamon, sugar, and salt into a large bowl. Add oatmeal and stir. Rub in butter with your fingers until mixture forms soft granules. Add raisins. Mix egg yolk and yogurt together. Add to flour mixture and stir until dough forms. Place dough on a floured board and knead several times. Cut dough in half. Form a flattened ball with each half. Cut into 6 wedges each. Brush each wedge with egg white and sprinkle with sugar. Place on an ungreased cookie sheet. Bake for 20 to 25 minutes. *Makes 12 scones.*

24

⌐ BLUEBERRY MUFFINS ⌐

3 *cups all-purpose flour*
2 *teaspoons baking soda*
2 *teaspoons baking powder*
1 *teaspoon salt*
½ *cup sugar*
4 *eggs*
6 *tablespoons butter, melted*
1 *cup milk*
1½ *cups blueberries, rinsed*
     and with stems removed

Preheat oven to 350°F. Sift together flour, baking soda, baking powder, salt, and sugar. In a separate bowl, mix eggs, butter, and milk. Add flour mixture to egg mixture. Mix just until ingredients are combined. Add blueberries. Spoon batter into greased muffin tins until each cup is ⅔ full. Bake for 15 to 20 minutes. Let cool in tins for 10 minutes before removing. *Makes 2 dozen muffins.*

⌒ APPLE BRAN MUFFINS ⌒

1½ cups all-purpose flour,
   sifted
1 teaspoon salt
4 teaspoons baking powder
1 tablespoon nutmeg
1 cup milk
1 egg
1½ cups bran
⅔ cup brown sugar
⅓ cup butter (⅔ stick),
   melted
4 small apples, peeled and
   diced

Preheat oven to 375°F. Sift together flour, salt, baking powder, and nutmeg. In a mixing bowl, beat together milk and egg. Add bran, brown sugar, and flour mixture. Mix in melted butter. Finally, fold in apple pieces. Spoon batter into greased muffin tins until each cup is ⅔ full. Bake for 15 to 20 minutes, or until a toothpick comes out clean. Let cool in tins for 10 minutes before removing. *Makes 12 muffins.*

CRUMPETS

1½ cups all-purpose flour
1 teaspoon sugar
1 teaspoon salt
1 ounce yeast
1¾ cups warm milk
⅔ cup warm water
2 eggs

Sift together flour, sugar, and salt in a bowl. Dissolve yeast in warm milk and add to the flour mixture. Mix in water and eggs. Beat hard to form a smooth batter. Cover and leave in a warm place for a half hour. Beat again thoroughly and leave to stand in a warm place for another half hour. Repeat this process once more. Place a greased frying pan over low heat. Place several crumpet rings in the pan. Spoon 2 tablespoons of batter into each ring. Leave for 6 minutes, or until underside is brown, then turn the rings over carefully and brown the other side. Transfer to a wire rack. Let cool, then remove rings and repeat process until batter is used up. *Makes 12 to 18 crumpets.*

Jams and Butters

"Don't forget the butter for
The Royal slice of bread."
The Alderney
Said sleepily:
"You'd better tell
His Majesty
That many people nowadays
Like marmalade
Instead."
  When We Were Very Young

STRAWBERRY JAM

2 cups ripe strawberries, rinsed
and hulled
1/3 cup sugar
juice of 1 lemon

Mash half of the strawberries and slice the other half thinly. Put all berries into a small pan, add sugar and lemon juice, and cook for a few minutes over medium heat, stirring constantly, until the mixture comes to a boil. Spoon the jam into a small crock or jar and allow to cool completely before refrigerating. If stored tightly covered in the refrigerator, jam will keep for 5 to 7 days.

ORANGE MARMALADE

3 *large oranges*
2 *lemons*
2 *tablespoons cornstarch*
3 *cups water*
1 *cup sugar*

Peel the oranges and lemons and slice peel into strips. Seed oranges and cut up pulp. Save peeled lemons for another use. Mix peels and orange pulp in a small bowl and set aside. In a saucepan, dissolve cornstarch in 1 cup of the water. Add orange mixture and cook, stirring constantly, for 2 to 3 minutes. Add sugar and the rest of the water and cook over medium heat, stirring constantly, until mixture thickens. Spoon marmalade into a small crock or jar and allow to cool completely before refrigerating. If stored tightly covered in the refrigerator, marmalade will keep for 5 to 7 days.

31

⮑ APPLE BUTTER ⮑

1 *pound McIntosh or Winesap apples (about 4 medium-size apples)*
1 *cup water*
½ *cup brown sugar*
1 *tablespoon lemon juice*
1 *tablespoon grated lemon rind*
1 *tablespoon cinnamon*
1 *tablespoon allspice*
2 *teaspoons nutmeg*

Cut apples into quarters, removing the core but not the peel. Place in a saucepan with water and simmer over medium heat until apples are soft. Put pulp through a strainer. Add sugar, lemon juice, lemon rind, cinnamon, allspice, and nutmeg. Place over low heat and stir constantly for about an hour, or until fruit butter thickens. To test for thickness, put a spoonful on a plate; if no rim of water forms, then the butter is done. Place in a sealed container and refrigerate; will keep for several weeks.

⌒ HONEY BUTTER ⌒

½ cup butter (1 stick)
3 tablespoons honey

Let butter stand until it is very soft. Then place it into a small bowl, cream it, add the honey, and mix thoroughly. Store tightly covered in the refrigerator; will keep for several weeks. Serve on scones, crumpets, or toast.

⌒ STRAWBERRY BUTTER ⌒

½ cup butter (1 stick)
4 large ripe strawberries,
 rinsed and hulled

Let butter stand until it is very soft. Then place it into a small bowl and cream it. Puree the strawberries and add them to the butter. Mix thoroughly. Store tightly covered in the refrigerator; will keep for several weeks. Serve on scones, muffins, crumpets, or pancakes.

33

Sandwiches

Kanga had sent them out with a
packet of watercress sandwiches for Roo and a packet of
extract-of-malt sandwiches for Tigger, to have a nice long
morning in the Forest not getting into mischief.
And off they had gone.
The House At Pooh Corner

35

⌒ CHICKEN SALAD ⌒

¾ cup mayonnaise

½ cup chopped celery

2 tablespoons dill weed

1 teaspoon ground black pepper

1 teaspoon dry mustard
(optional)

2 cups diced cooked chicken

8 slices whole-wheat or white
bread

In a bowl, mix together mayonnaise, celery, dill, black pepper, mustard, and chicken. Assemble sandwiches and cut diagonally. *Makes 8 small sandwiches.*

➤ CURRIED CHICKEN SALAD ➤

1 cup plain yogurt
2 tablespoons curry powder
¼ cup raisins
¼ cup shredded apple
2 cups diced cooked chicken
8 slices whole-wheat or white bread

Warm yogurt in microwave or on top of stove. Stir in curry powder, raisins, shredded apple, and chicken. Let cool. Assemble sandwiches and cut diagonally. *Makes 8 small sandwiches.*

⌒ EGG SALAD ⌒

4 hard-boiled eggs
¼ cup mayonnaise
2 tablespoons prepared
  horseradish
2 tablespoons minced onion
8 slices whole-wheat or white
  bread

Chop eggs as finely as possible. Add mayonnaise, horseradish, and onion. Mix thoroughly. Assemble sandwiches and cut diagonally. *Makes 8 small sandwiches.*

ᴄ CUCUMBER SANDWICHES ᴄ

½ to 1 cup lemon juice
1 teaspoon salt
1 teaspoon ground black pepper
½ medium-size cucumber
8 slices soft white bread
butter, for buttering bread
watercress, for garnish

Pour lemon juice into a small shallow pan or dish. Add salt and pepper. Peel cucumber. Slice thinly, crosswise. Lay cucumber slices in lemon mixture and let soak. Be sure to turn cucumber slices over after a few minutes so both sides are soaked. Trim the crusts from the bread. Lay the bread on a wooden board and use a rolling pin to flatten. Butter the bread lightly. Drain cucumber slices and lay generously on 4 slices of bread. Assemble the sandwiches and cut diagonally. Serve with a watercress garnish. *Makes 8 small sandwiches.*

⮜ HAM SANDWICHES WITH HONEY MUSTARD ⮞

4 tablespoons prepared mustard

2 tablespoons honey

6 slices whole-wheat or white bread

6 pieces thinly sliced ham

In a small bowl, combine mustard and honey and mix well. Spread honey-mustard sauce on 3 slices of bread and lay 2 slices of ham on each. Assemble sandwiches. Cut each sandwich into 4 strips. *Makes 12 small sandwiches.*

⌒ TUNA SALAD ⌒

1 six-ounce can of tuna,
 drained
3 tablespoons mayonnaise
4 to 6 black olives, finely
 chopped
2 tablespoons minced onion
6 slices whole-wheat or white
 bread
tomato, thinly sliced (optional)
lettuce, shredded (optional)

Place tuna in a bowl, add mayonnaise, olives, and onion, and mix thoroughly. Assemble sandwiches (with thin slices of tomato or shredded lettuce, if desired) and cut each into 4 strips. *Makes 12 small sandwiches.*

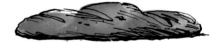

CREAM CHEESE SPREAD

8 ounces soft cream cheese
3 tablespoons Worcestershire
    sauce
1 tablespoon soy sauce
2 tablespoons garlic powder
8 slices whole-wheat bread
tomato, thinly sliced (optional)
cucumber, peeled and thinly
    sliced (optional)

Mash cream cheese with a spoon. When soft and fluffy, add Worcestershire sauce, soy sauce, and garlic powder. Mix well. Spread the cream cheese mixture onto 4 slices of whole-wheat bread, add tomato or cucumber, if desired, and top with 4 more slices of bread. Cut into quarters. *Makes 16 small sandwiches.*

⌒ BANANA-HONEY SANDWICHES ⌒

1 *large ripe banana*
6 *slices whole-wheat bread*
2 *to 4 tablespoons honey*

Slice the banana into thin rounds and place the rounds on three slices of bread. Spread honey on the other three slices of bread. Assemble the sandwiches, cut into triangle wedges, and serve. *Makes 12 small sandwiches.*

Cookies and Biscuits

Pooh took down a very large jar of honey
from the top shelf. It had HUNNY written on it, but,
just to make sure, he took off the paper cover and looked at it,
and it *looked* just like honey. "But you never can
tell," said Pooh. So he put his tongue in, and
took a large lick. "Yes," he said, "it is.
And honey, I should say, right down to the bottom."

Winnie-the-Pooh

JAM COOKIES

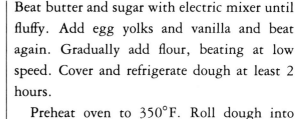

1 cup butter (2 sticks)
1/2 cup sugar
2 egg yolks
1 teaspoon vanilla extract
2 1/2 cups all-purpose flour
1/3 cup strawberry jam

Beat butter and sugar with electric mixer until fluffy. Add egg yolks and vanilla and beat again. Gradually add flour, beating at low speed. Cover and refrigerate dough at least 2 hours.

Preheat oven to 350°F. Roll dough into 1-inch balls and place 1 inch apart on ungreased cookie sheets. Make an indentation in the center of each ball and fill with jam. Bake for 15 minutes, or until golden. *Makes 3 to 4 dozen cookies.*

⌒ LEMON BARS ⌒

CRUST:

1 cup butter (2 sticks)

2 cups all-purpose flour

½ cup powdered sugar

FILLING:

4 eggs

½ teaspoon freshly grated lemon
rind

½ teaspoon baking powder

⅓ cup lemon juice

¼ cup all-purpose flour

2 cups granulated sugar

powdered sugar, for decoration

Preheat oven to 350°F. Mix together butter, flour, and sugar until a rich dough forms. Spread in a well-greased 9 × 13-inch pan. Bake for 20 to 25 minutes. Cool for 10 minutes.

Beat eggs. Slowly mix in lemon rind, baking powder, lemon juice, flour, and sugar. Pour mixture over cooked crust. Bake at 350°F for 20 to 25 minutes. Cool in pan for 30 minutes. Dust with powdered sugar and cut into bars. *Makes 2 dozen bars.*

47

⌒ ALMOND COOKIES ⌒

1½ cups all-purpose flour
rind of 1 lemon, finely grated
½ cup butter (1 stick)
½ cup sugar
2 egg yolks
½ cup ground almonds

Preheat oven to 350°F. Sift flour and add lemon rind. In another bowl, cream butter and sugar until fluffy. Add egg yolks and beat. Gradually stir in flour mixture. Stir in almonds. Roll out dough to thickness of ¼ inch. Cut with cookie cutter. Bake on greased cookie sheets for 8 to 10 minutes, or until golden. *Makes 2 dozen cookies.*

✑ WALNUT DIAMONDS ✑

CRUST:
½ cup butter (1 stick)
1½ cups all-purpose flour
¼ cup ice water

FILLING:
1½ cups brown sugar
1 cup butter (2 sticks)
½ cup honey
⅓ cup sugar
1 pound shelled walnuts,
   coarsely chopped
¼ cup heavy cream

Cut butter into flour until it resembles coarse meal. Add water and mix. Gather dough into a ball and chill 1 hour. Butter and flour a 9 × 13-inch pan. Roll out dough and fit into pan. Pierce with fork.

Preheat oven to 400°F. Bring brown sugar, butter, honey, and sugar to a boil in a saucepan, stirring constantly. Boil for about 4 minutes until thick and dark. Remove from heat and stir in walnuts. Add cream and blend. Pour mixture over dough and bake for about 25 minutes, or until edges are golden. Cool. Cut diagonally across the pan to form diamonds. *Makes 2 dozen cookies.*

49

⁀ SHORTBREAD ⁀

2 cups all-purpose flour
1/2 cup cornmeal
1/4 teaspoon baking powder
1 cup butter (2 sticks)
1/2 cup powdered sugar
2 drops almond extract
granulated or powdered sugar,
  for decoration

Preheat oven to 325°F. Sift together flour, cornmeal, and baking powder in one bowl. In a separate bowl, cream together butter, sugar, and almond extract. Add flour mixture and blend until dough is light and crumbly. Press dough evenly into 2 greased 9-inch round cake pans. Decorate by pricking with a fork, creating the outline of 8 pie wedges. Bake for 20 to 25 minutes, or until golden brown. Remove from oven and sprinkle lightly with granulated or powdered sugar. Cool in tins for 5 to 10 minutes before cutting and serving. Cut along lines created with fork. *Serves 16.*

⌒ SUGAR COOKIES ⌒

4¼ cups all-purpose flour
1 teaspoon salt
1 teaspoon baking soda
1 teaspoon cream of tartar
1 cup butter (2 sticks)
1 cup powdered sugar
1 cup granulated sugar
1 cup vegetable oil
2 eggs
granulated sugar, for
   decoration

Preheat oven to 375°F. Sift together flour, salt, baking soda, and cream of tartar. Set aside. Melt butter in a saucepan. Mix together hot butter, powdered sugar, granulated sugar, vegetable oil, and eggs. Gradually add flour mixture. Blend until dough forms. Form dough into 1-inch balls and place on an ungreased cookie sheet. Flatten with the bottom of a glass that has been dipped in granulated sugar. Bake for 15 minutes, or until light brown. *Makes 4 dozen cookies.*

⌒ SHREWSBURY BISCUITS ⌒

¾ *cup butter (1½ sticks)*
¾ *cup powdered sugar*
1¼ *cups all-purpose flour,*
sifted
3 *tablespoons freshly grated*
lemon rind
⅓ *cup raisins*
powdered sugar, for decoration

Preheat oven to 350°F. Cream butter and sugar. Mix in flour, lemon rind, and raisins. Knead paste with floured hands in bowl for several minutes, until smooth. Lay on a floured board and roll out to thickness of ¼ inch. Cut out 2- to 3-inch circles. Place on 2 greased cookie sheets. Bake for 15 minutes. Immediately sprinkle with powdered sugar. Allow to cool for 5 minutes on cookie sheets before placing on rack. *Makes 12 to 18 biscuits.*

52

CHOCOLATE DIGESTIVES

1 cup all-purpose flour
1½ cups whole-wheat flour
¼ cup bran
½ teaspoon baking powder
½ teaspoon baking soda
½ teaspoon salt
½ cup butter (1 stick), chilled
¾ cup brown sugar
1 egg, beaten
½ cup water
6 ounces semisweet chocolate

Preheat oven to 375°F. Mix flours, bran, baking powder, baking soda, and salt. Cut in butter until it is in small bits. Add sugar and stir. Add egg and water and mix until batter forms a soft dough. Place on a floured surface and knead until smooth dough is formed. Roll out dough to thickness of ⅛ inch. Cut into 2-inch rounds and bake on greased cookie sheets for 8 to 10 minutes, or until lightly browned. Melt chocolate in microwave or in double boiler. Spread chocolate over cooled biscuits. *Makes about 5 dozen digestives.*

Cakes and Pastries

"Pooh," Owl said, "Christopher Robin is giving a party."
"Oh!" said Pooh. And then seeing that Owl expected
him to say something else, he said, "Will there be
those little cake things with pink sugar icing?"
Owl felt that it was rather beneath him to talk about
little cake things with pink sugar icing.
Winnie-the-Pooh

⌒ HONEY CAKE ⌒

1¾ cups all-purpose flour
½ cup sugar
2 teaspoons baking powder
1 teaspoon salt
1 teaspoon cinnamon
½ cup milk
2 eggs
½ cup butter (1 stick),
   softened
½ teaspoon vanilla extract
¼ cup honey
powdered sugar, for decoration

Preheat oven to 375°F. Sift dry ingredients together. While mixing, slowly add milk, eggs, softened butter, vanilla, and honey. When a creamy batter has formed, pour into 2 greased 9-inch round cake pans. Bake for 20 to 25 minutes, or until brown around the edges. Sprinkle with powdered sugar and allow to cool for 10 minutes in pan before serving. *Serves 12.*

☞ CARROT CAKE ☜

CAKE:

2 cups all-purpose flour
2 teaspoons baking soda
3/4 tablespoon salt
1 tablespoon cinnamon
2 cups granulated sugar
4 eggs
1 1/2 cups vegetable oil
1 cup chopped pecans
2 cups coarsely grated carrots

FROSTING:

1 pound cream cheese
2 teaspoons vanilla extract
1/2 cup butter (1 stick)
1 3/4 cups powdered sugar

Preheat oven to 350°F. Sift together flour, baking soda, salt, and cinnamon. Set aside. Cream sugar and eggs together. Add flour mixture and oil, alternately. Fold in pecans and carrots. Pour batter into 2 thoroughly greased 8-inch round cake pans. Bake for 40 minutes. Cool in cake pans for 15 minutes. Carefully remove and cool on wire rack before frosting.

Mix cream cheese, vanilla, butter, and powdered sugar. Spread between layers and on top of cake. *Serves 12.*

☞ LEMON POPPY-SEED CAKES ☜

⅔ cup cake flour (not self-rising)
½ teaspoon baking soda
¼ cup butter (½ stick)
½ cup sugar
2 eggs
2 tablespoons lemon juice
1 teaspoon vanilla extract
2 teaspoons grated lemon zest
2 tablespoons poppy seeds
¼ cup plain yogurt
powdered sugar, for decoration

Preheat oven to 375°F. Sift flour and baking soda into a bowl. In another bowl, cream butter and sugar. Add eggs, lemon juice, vanilla, lemon zest, and poppy seeds and beat well. Add flour mixture and mix well. Add yogurt and mix again. Spoon batter into buttered and floured muffin tins until each cup is ⅔ full. Bake for 15 to 20 minutes, or until golden. If desired, dust with powdered sugar. *Makes 6 to 8 cakes.*

LEMON POUND CAKE

1 cup butter (2 sticks)
1½ cups sugar
6 eggs
2 cups cake flour (not self-rising)
½ teaspoon salt
2 tablespoons lemon juice
2 teaspoons grated lemon zest

Preheat oven to 325°F. Let refrigerated ingredients come to room temperature. Cream butter and sugar until well combined. Add eggs, one at a time, and beat until smooth. Add flour and salt and beat. Add lemon juice and zest and mix well. Pour batter into a greased and floured 9 × 5 × 3-inch loaf pan and smooth top. Bake for 1¼ hours, or until tester comes out clean. Cool in pan on rack.

CHOCOLATE CAKE

CAKE:

1½ cups all-purpose flour
3 tablespoons cocoa
1 cup granulated sugar
1 teaspoon baking soda
½ teaspoon salt
6 tablespoons butter, melted
1 tablespoon vinegar
1 teaspoon vanilla extract
1 cup water

FROSTING:

8 ounces cream cheese
1 teaspoon vanilla extract
¼ cup butter (½ stick)
1 cup powdered sugar

Preheat oven to 350°F. Sift flour, cocoa, sugar, baking soda, and salt into a bowl. Add melted butter, vinegar, and vanilla. Add water and stir until ingredients are barely combined. Pour batter into a greased 8 × 8-inch pan and bake for 35 to 40 minutes. Let cool for 10 minutes, then remove from pan. Cool completely before frosting.

Mix cream cheese, vanilla, butter, and powdered sugar. Spread over cooled cake.

⌒ ECCLES CAKES ⌒

1 cup currants
¼ cup raisins
⅔ cup sugar
2 sheets puff pastry (if frozen,
    thaw as directed on
    package)
milk, for brushing over cakes
sugar, for dredging cakes

Preheat oven to 425°F. Combine currants and raisins, cover with boiling water, and steep for a few minutes. Drain, add sugar, and mix well. Cut 4-inch rounds from pastry dough. Place a spoonful of the currant mixture in center of each round, moisten the edges, fold over, and press closed. Roll closed cake to flatten slightly, brush with milk, and dredge in sugar. Arrange cakes on a greased cookie sheet and bake for 12 to 15 minutes, or until golden. *Makes 12 to 16 cakes.*

☙ MERINGUES ☙

4 egg whites
¼ teaspoon cream of tartar
1 teaspoon vanilla extract
1 cup sugar
4 drops red food coloring
   (optional)

Preheat oven to 225°F. In a small bowl, beat egg whites until they form stiff peaks. Add cream of tartar and vanilla. Add sugar 2 tablespoons at a time, beating for a minute after each addition. Add food coloring (just enough to give mixture a light pink color) and beat for 15 seconds. Total beating time should be about 10 minutes, after which meringue should be stiff and glossy. Drop generous spoonfuls of meringue about 1 inch apart onto 2 baking sheets lined with greased waxed paper. Bake for 1 hour, or until light brown. Turn off the oven, but leave meringues inside for another hour. *Makes 2 to 3 dozen meringues.*

PECAN TARTS

DOUGH:

1 cup butter (2 sticks)
8 ounces cream cheese
2 cups all-purpose flour

FILLING:

3 eggs, slightly beaten
1½ cups light brown sugar
1½ cups chopped pecans
3 tablespoons butter, melted
2 teaspoons vanilla extract

Let butter and cream cheese stand until soft. Cream them together, add flour gradually, and mix well. Roll dough into walnut-size balls. Press each into a cup of a minimuffin tin, leaving a depression at the center and a lip of dough at top.

Preheat oven to 350°F. Combine eggs, brown sugar, pecans, butter, and vanilla. Fill dough cups almost full. Bake for 25 minutes, or until golden. *Makes 3 to 4 dozen tarts.*

63

Index